Jeb's Barn

Written by Andrea Butler
Illustrated by Hannu Taina

📖 GoodYearBooks

At eight o'clock on Monday,

everyone went to Jeb's farm
to build a barn.

At ten o'clock on Tuesday,

4

they put up the frame.

At twelve o'clock on Wednesday,

they put up the walls.

At two o'clock on Thursday,

8

they put on the roof.

At four o'clock on Friday,

they put on the doors and shutters.

11

At six o'clock on Saturday,

they led the animals in.

At eight o'clock on Sunday,
they had a special dinner.

Jeb's brother said,
"I need a new barn too."

So. . . .